Rosy's Visitors

Judy Hindley

illustrated by Helen Craig

WALKER BOOKS
AND SUBSIDIARIES
LONDON • BOSTON • SYDNEY

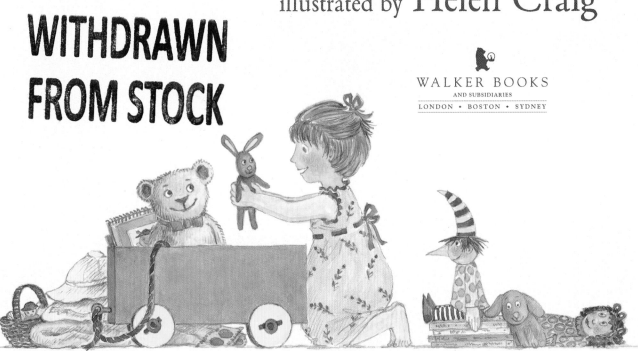

One day Rosy said,
"Today is moving day.
I'm going to find myself
a whole new house."
She packed up her blanket
and her pillow, and her
books and toys, and
all her favourite things …
and started looking.

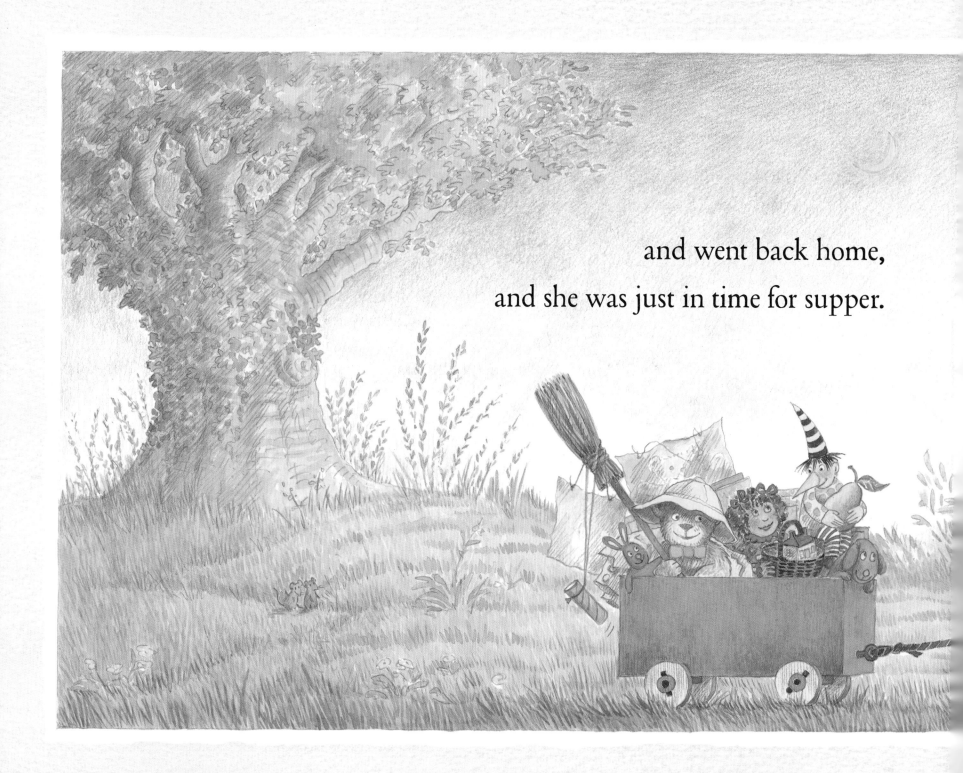

and went back home,
and she was just in time for supper.

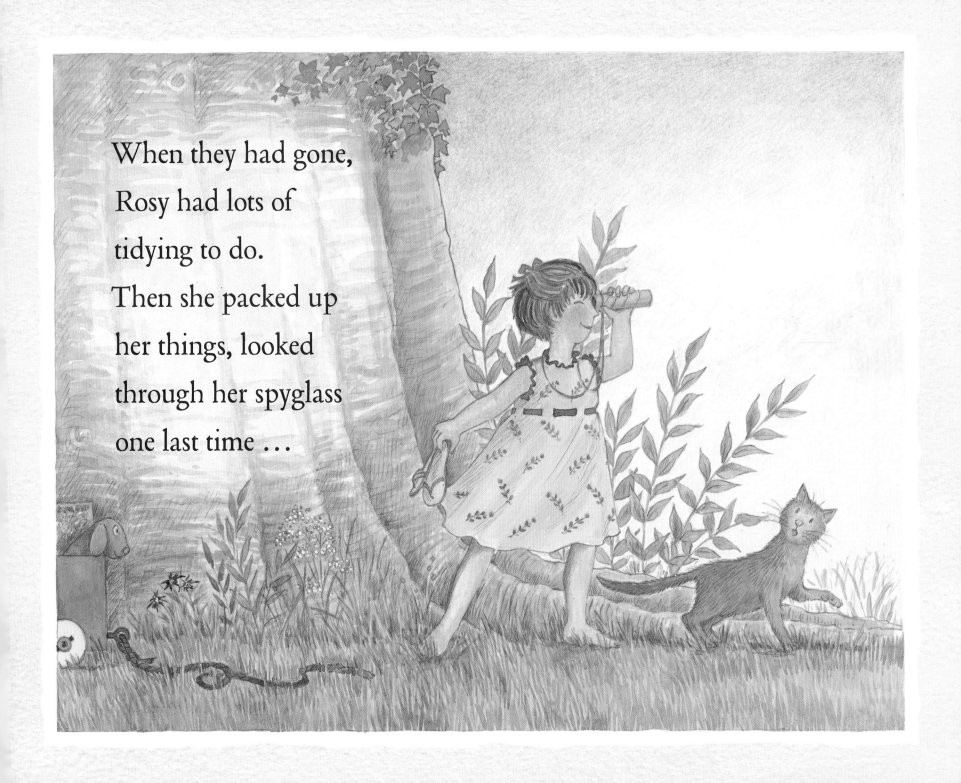

When they had gone,
Rosy had lots of
tidying to do.
Then she packed up
her things, looked
through her spyglass
one last time …

till they were so tired out they had to leave.

"Goodbye! Goodbye!" they called.

"Come again!" cried Rosy.

Then
they came
in the house and
tried out everything.
They all loved Rosy's house.
They had a tremendous feast,
and they sang and they danced …

"Welcome to my house!" cried Rosy.
Rosy's visitors came up the path
and rang the bell, and said hello.
They bowed and curtsied, and they
all brought gifts because
it was their first visit.

ROSY'S HOUSE

And there they were.

There were Rosy's visitors, coming in
from the sea, and down from the sky,
and all across the land …
to Rosy's house.

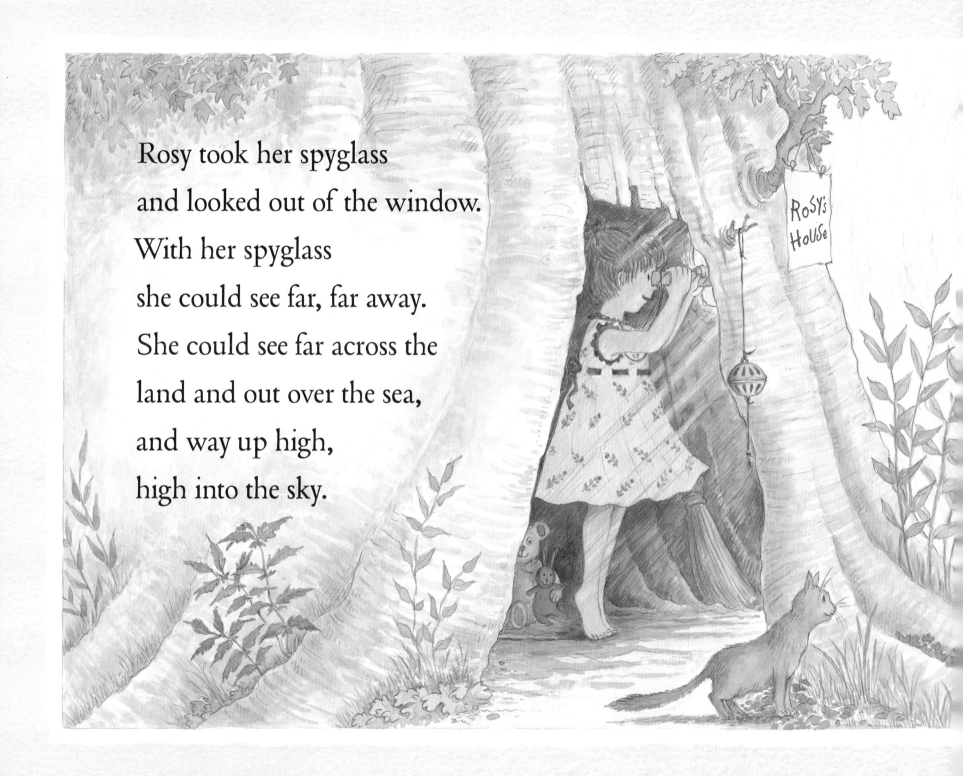

Rosy took her spyglass
and looked out of the window.
With her spyglass
she could see far, far away.
She could see far across the
land and out over the sea,
and way up high,
high into the sky.

Then she said, "Now I need a bell for visitors to ring." She found a jingle-bell and hung it by the door. "There!" she said. "Now everything is perfect. I'm ready for visitors. I wonder if anyone will come."

"Hmm," said Rosy. "I wonder if visitors
will find my house. I think I just need
a path, so visitors can find the way."
She found some stones
and things, and marked
a path right up to
her front door.

When she was finished,
Rosy clapped her hands.
"This is my house,
it's Rosy's house!"
she sang.
And she put up a sign
so everyone could
see that this was
Rosy's house.

She hung up her coat and
rain hat and she made her bed.
She found a special place to
sit and think, or draw,
or read her book.

Rosy got busy.
"This is my house; it's mine,
all mine!" she sang.
She swept and
tidied her
house, and
made it neat.

Very soon she found a little house.
She peeked in through the door.
She looked all around.
"This is it! This is my house!"
cried Rosy. "What a
perfect house."